Tommy Lasorda

Always Room for One More

Always Room for One More

by Sorche Nic Leodhas

Illustrated by Nonny Hogrogian

Henry Holt and Company
New York

ISBN 0-8050-0331-2 (hardcover)
7 9 11 13 15 14 12 10 8
ISBN 0-8050-0330-4 (paperback)
7 9 11 13 15 14 12 10 8

Printed in the United States of America

ISBN 0-8050-0331-2 HARDCOVER
ISBN 0-8050-0330-4 PAPERBACK

And This One for
Allan Digby
Toiseach an fhine againne

Books for Young People By Sorche Nic Leodhas

ALWAYS ROOM FOR ONE MORE
GHOSTS GO HAUNTING
GAELIC GHOSTS
ALL IN THE MORNING EARLY
THISTLE AND THYME
HEATHER AND BROOM

Always Room for One More

1.

There was a wee house in the heather—
    'Twas a bit o' a but and a ben—
And in it there lived all together
    Lachie MacLachlan
        And his good wife,
            And his bairns to the number of ten.
"There's a fire on the hearthstone to warm me,
    And porridge to spare in the pot,"
Said Lachie. "The weather is stormy,
    So me and my wife
        And our ten bairns,
            Will be sharing whatever we've got."

So he hailed every traveler that passed by his door.
Said Lachie MacLachlan, "There's room galore.
Och, come awa' in! There's room for one more,
Always room for one more!"

A tinker came first, then a tailor,
  And a sailor with line and lead;
A gallowglass and a fishing lass,
  With a creel o' fish on her head;
A merry auld wife full o' banter,
  Four peat-cutters up from the bog,
Piping Rury the Ranter,
    And a shepherd laddie
      Down from the brae,
        With his canny wee shepherd dog.

He hailed them all in as he stood at the door.
Said Lachie MacLachlan, "There's room galore.
Och, come awa' in! There's room for one more,
Always room for one more!"

2.

Rury's pipes set the rafters a-ringing
   Till the clock danced a reel on the shelf,
And they all fell to dancing and singing,
   And the little dog danced by himself.
Och, the walls they bulged out and bulged in then,
   The walls they bulged in and out.
There will never be heard such a din, then,
   As came from the folks
     In the wee little house
      While they rollicked and frolicked about.

They filled all the house up from door to door,
But Lachie cried out, "There's room galore.
'Twould be a tight fit, but there's room for one more,
Always room for one more!"

Then the rafters they clappit like thunder,
  And folks in the nearby town
Stood stock-still to listen and wonder,
  When the wee little house
    With its but and its ben
      And its walls and its roof DINGED DOWN!
Then the tinker and the tailor,
  And the sailor with line and lead;
The gallowglass, and the fishing lass,
  With the creel o' fish on her head;
The auld wife full o' banter,
  The four peat-cutters up from the bog,

3.

Piping Rury the Ranter,
   And the shepherd laddie down from the brae,
With his canny wee shepherd dog,
        AND

          Lachie MacLachlan,
            His good wife,
              And his bairns to the number of ten,
             They all tumbled out again!

    And they gowked at the place where the house stood before.
      "Och, Lachie," they cried, "there was room galore,
    But worry and woe, there's no room no more,
      Never no room no more!"

They wailed for a while in the heather,
  As glum as a grumpetie grouse,
Then they shouted, "Have done with this blether!
For Lachie MacLachlan,
  His wife and bairns,
    We'll raise up a bonny new house."
The house that they raised from the auld one
  Was double as wide and as high.
Should an army come by it could hauld one,
  With Lachie MacLachlan,
    His wife and bairns,
      And whoever else happened by.

And then the whole lot of them stood at the door,
And merrily shouted, "There's room galore!
Now there will always be room for one more,
Always room for one more!"

ABOUT THE STORY

Sorche Nic Leodhas says that:

"ALWAYS ROOM FOR ONE MORE is one of the many Scottish popular songs which have been preserved by oral tradition, being handed down by one generation to the next, but never appearing in print. My father sang it to us when we were children. He had been taught it by his father when he was a little boy, and my grandfather remembered it from his own early childhood. Because the Scottish words in which this merry little tune was written are somewhat difficult to understand, it was necessary to change many of them into others more familiar to American boys and girls. However, some of the Scottish words were left in the song because they sounded better than any new ones I might choose, and for those who would like an explanation of them, I have provided their definitions here:

A bit o' a but and a ben • *A big room and a little room. Usually it means a front room (a but) in which most of the family living is carried on and a smaller extra room (a ben) built on behind.*

Bairns • *Children midway in age between weans, who are very, very small; and lads and lasses, who are well on the way toward growing up.*

Brae • *A brae is a grassy hillside. Shepherds herd their sheep there because there is plenty of grass for the flocks.*

Come awa' in • *This is really 'Come away in.' Scots use many English words but pronounce them in their own way. This is a friendly, cordial way of inviting a person to come in. Americans say 'Come right in!' to mean the same thing.*

Gallowglass • *A mercenary soldier. That means one who hires himself out to fight in the army of any country which will pay him for it. We sometimes call these men 'soldiers of fortune' nowadays. The word is made up of two Gaelic words, 'gall' meaning stranger, and 'gleaich' meaning fighting servant. So it means literally, one who serves the stranger in a battle.*

Clappit • *Made a loud explosive noise. In English we speak of a thunderclap, as this sort of sound made by thunder. Where in English -ed is used to form the past tense of a verb, in Scots -it is added to the verb.*

Canny • *This is a word of many meanings. In the song it means clever. It can also mean sly, or wary, or wise.*

Dinged down • *Tumbled down, banged down, crashed down with a great, big noise.*

Gowked • *Stared at something in silly fashion. A gowk is a cuckoo which is supposed to be a silly bird.*

Grumpetie grouse • *A broody grouse—one that looks very sulky, with its head down and its feathers all ruffled.*

Blether • *Foolish talk.*

Och • *The Scottish way of saying 'Oh.' "*

Note about the song

Like many folk songs, this one was partly told and partly sung. We have given the tune for the first verse and chorus; the singer will find that he will want to adapt it himself to the rest of the verses. A flexible and individual use of this basic little tune is essential to a happy rendering of ALWAYS ROOM FOR ONE MORE.

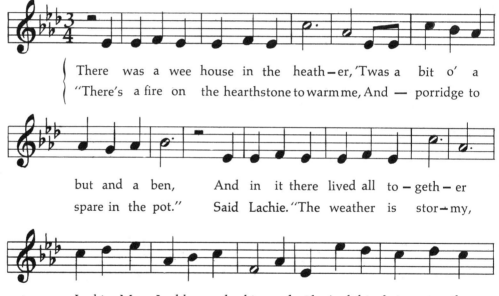

There was a wee house in the heath—er, 'Twas a bit o' a
"There's a fire on the hearthstone to warm me, And — porridge to

but and a ben, And in it there lived all to — geth — er
spare in the pot." Said Lachie. "The weather is stor—my,

Lachie Mac—Lachlan and his good wife And his bairns to the
So me and my wife And our ten bairns Will be shar—ing what

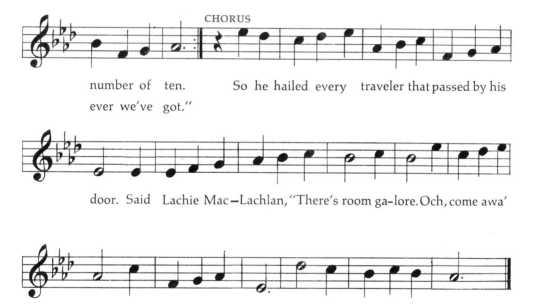

number of ten.   So he hailed every   traveler that passed by his
ever we've got."

door. Said   Lachie Mac—Lachlan, "There's room ga-lore. Och, come awa'

in! There's room for one   more,   Al—ways room for one more."